Then I Think of God

WRITTEN BY Martha Whitmore Hickman

ILLUSTRATED BY Higgins Bond

ALBERT WHITMAN & COMPANY

Morton Grove, Illinois

Also by Martha Whitmore Hickman:

And God Created Squash: How the World Began

A Baby Born in Bethlehem

Robert Lives with His Grandparents

When Andy's Father Went to Prison

Library of Congress Cataloging-in-Publication Data

Hickman, Martha Whitmore
Then I think of God / by Martha Whitmore Hickman; illustrated by Higgins Bond.
p. cm.
Summary: Children describe moments in their lives when their thoughts turn to God.
ISBN 0-8075-7847-9 (hardcover)
[1. God—Fiction.] I. Title. PZ7.H53143 Th 2003 [E]—dc21 2002011545

Published in 2003 by Albert Whitman & Company,
6340 Oakton Street, Morton Grove, Illinois 60053-2723.
Published simultaneously in Canada by Fitzhenry & Whiteside, Markham, Ontario.
Printed in the United States of America.
10 9 8 7 6 5 4 3 2 1

The design is by Carol Gildar.
The text is set in Caxton.

For more information about Albert Whitman & Company,
visit our web site at www.albertwhitman.com.

To the pastors and people of
Edgehill United Methodist Church, Nashville, Tennessee.
M.W. H.

This is for my grandmother, Elizabeth Washington (1895–1982),
for her faith in me.
H.B.

When I'm running in the park with my dad, trying my new butterfly kite, and the kite just bumps along behind us, and then a giant wind comes and lifts it into the air and the string tugs at my hands . . .

and we stop running and watch the kite
dancing and swirling like a giant butterfly
against the blue sky . . .
then I think of God.

When the robin's eggs we've been
watching hatch and four baby birds stick their
heads up with their tiny mouths open for the
food their mother brings, and then in a few
days, one by one, they perch on the edge of the
nest and fly and they're a little wobbly at first,
but then they fly away out of sight and when it
gets dark they fly back to their nest like people
come back home to their houses . . .
then I think of God.

When I'm sitting with my mom and dad in church and the organ is playing very softly and it's a song I know and everyone is quietly listening and so am I . . .
I think of God.

When the first leaves from the sunflower seeds come pushing up through the dirt and my mom shows me which plants are the weeds and we pull them up carefully . . .

and one day we go out and the stems have grown tall and the green buds have opened to flowers with dark centers and great yellow petals, and I wonder how the sunflowers could grow so big and so fast . . .

then I think of God.

When my friend Grace gets so sick she
has to stay in bed for two weeks and she has to
miss my birthday party and I can't even go and
see her (but we send her some cake), and then
she has to go to the hospital and I miss her and
I wonder if she's ever going to be okay . . .
I think of God.

When Grace gets better and she comes
home again, and we can sit on her porch and
look at books and make funny animals out of clay
and she laughs a lot just like she used to . . .
I think of God.

When my mom and dad bring our new baby home from the hospital, and she was in my mother's tummy and I could feel her but we couldn't even see her, and now I get to hold her on my lap and she smiles at me like she already knows I'm her big brother . . . then I think of God.

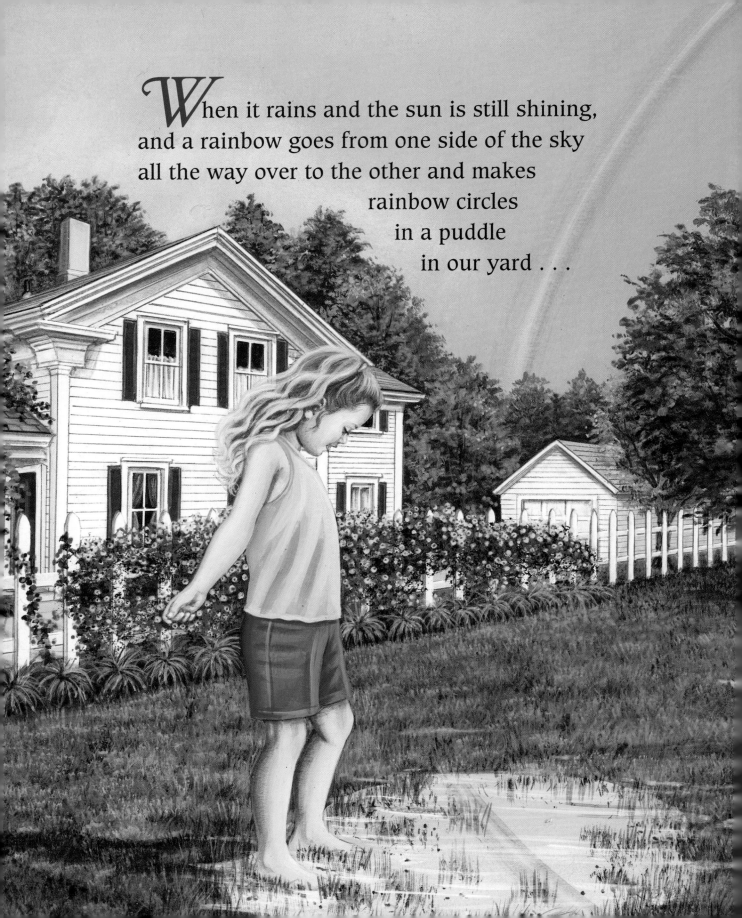

When it rains and the sun is still shining,
and a rainbow goes from one side of the sky
all the way over to the other and makes
rainbow circles
in a puddle
in our yard . . .

I think of God.

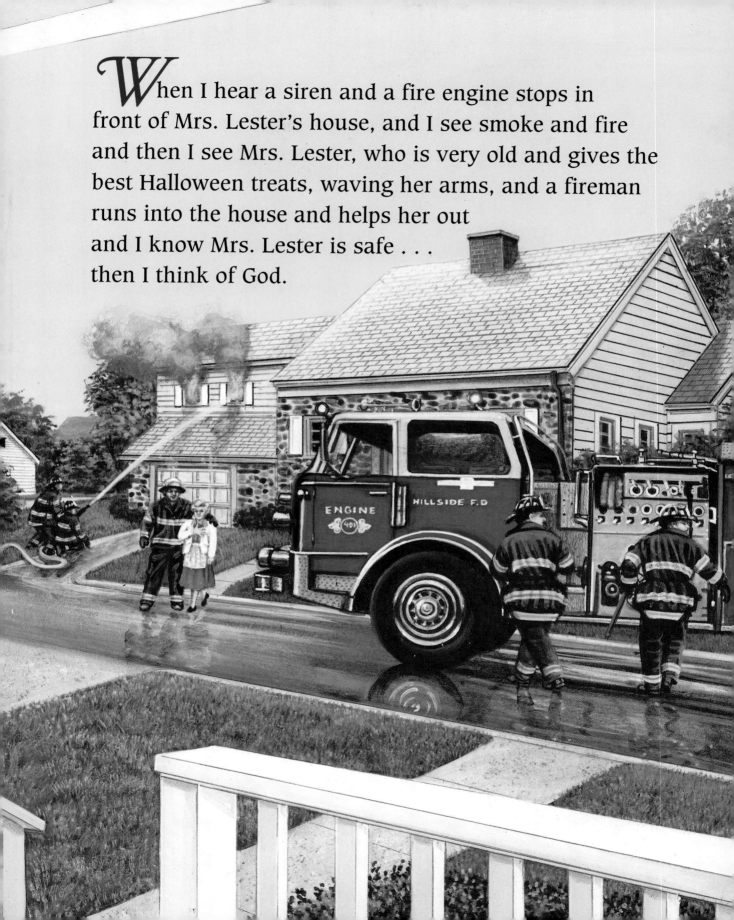

When I hear a siren and a fire engine stops in front of Mrs. Lester's house, and I see smoke and fire and then I see Mrs. Lester, who is very old and gives the best Halloween treats, waving her arms, and a fireman runs into the house and helps her out and I know Mrs. Lester is safe . . . then I think of God.

When a boy from South America moves into our neighborhood and he doesn't understand English, and the kids on the other team don't choose him and at first we don't either but then we do, and the first time Juan's up at bat, he hits a home run and we cheer and cheer and rush up and give him high-fives, and he says, "*Gracias, gracias*," and he's smiling, which I never saw him do before, and I feel like crying and laughing at the same time . . .
then I think of God.

When winter comes and Jimmy and Juan and I
go out to play in the snow, and Jimmy and I start to
throw snowballs but Juan, who has never seen
snow, keeps saying, *"¡Qué hermosa!"* which means
"how beautiful," and Jimmy and I stop our snowball
fight and see how the snow has made beautiful
shining mountains of our bushes . . .
then I think of God.

After I say my prayers and my mom and dad kiss me goodnight, and Zingo is right next to me and I know that pretty soon I'll be sound asleep . . .

then I think of God.